JAKE MADDOX

EXTREME ICE ADVENTURE

BY JAKE MADDOX

Text by Salima Alikhan

Illustrated by Giuliano Aloisi and Alan Brown

STONE ARCH BOOKS
a capstone imprint

Jake Maddox Adventure is published by Stone Arch Books,
an imprint of Capstone.
1710 Roe Crest Drive
North Mankato, Minnesota 56003
www.capstonepub.com

Library of Congress Cataloging-in-Publication Data is available on the
Library of Congress website.

ISBN: 978-1-4965-8698-8 (hardcover)
ISBN: 978-1-4965-9205-7 (paperback)
ISBN: 978-1-4965-8699-5 (eBook PDF)

Summary: Nita and Sohail are thrilled when they win scholarships to
attend the Alaska Young Explorers competition. Both kids need the
prize money to help their families, but things take a turn when they
make a misstep while hiking down a glacier. The two find themselves
in dangerous territory and will have to work together if they want to
survive the Alaskan wilderness.

Cover illustration by Giuliano Aloisi

Designer: Lori Bye

Printed in the United States of America.
PA100

TABLE OF CONTENTS

CHAPTER 1

YOUNG EXPLORERS

"Think fast, Nita!" called Sohail Aman.

A snowball whizzed past Nita Dara's head. She ducked just in time. When she stood back up, Sohail was laughing.

Before Nita could make a snowball of her own, one of the Alaska Young Explorers guides interrupted.

"Listen up, everyone!" the guide called. "We have an exciting new challenge for you!"

Nita straightened up, breathing in the fresh Alaska air. She loved new challenges. It was one of the reasons she'd signed up for this adventure.

The Alaska Young Explorers—ten eighth graders in total—shuffled through the snow toward the guides. The crampons strapped to the bottoms of their boots struck the snow with soft *thunks* as the spikes pierced the frost.

Crampons made it easier to walk in the snow. They also gave everyone what looked like big, spiky monster feet, which was really cool.

"What's the new challenge?" one of the other kids called.

"Whatever it is, I plan on winning," Sohail spoke up. He was already winding up another snowball.

Nita rolled her eyes. *Everyone* wanted to win, of course. That was the whole reason they were there. Each kid had won a Young Explorers scholarship. The scholarship allowed kids who didn't have much money to visit a wilderness camp in Alaska to learn explorer skills.

But it was more than just a camp. It was a competition. That was the part Nita cared about the most. Whoever won the Alaska Young Explorers prize would be awarded *five thousand dollars.*

Nita could barely repeat the amount to herself without jittering. *Five thousand dollars.*

She'd first heard about the competition months ago. Her Aunt Carmen, who had raised her, had burst into their New York City apartment one day.

"Nita, I just heard about an opportunity you can't miss!" Aunt Carmen had announced. "You have to apply!"

And so Nita had. She'd filled out the application. Then she'd written an essay explaining some of the hardships she'd faced and why she thought she would make a great Alaska Young Explorer.

To her surprise, she'd been awarded a scholarship. A few months later, she'd boarded a plane to Alaska to be part of the competition.

Winning the Alaska Young Explorers prize would make Aunt Carmen proud, but it wasn't just about pride. Nita's family really, really needed the money. If Nita won, Aunt Carmen would finally be able to get her dental work done. And Nita would be able to buy the school supplies she needed.

And maybe our water won't get shut off so often, Nita thought. She gripped her ice ax, determined. She was *going* to win that money.

They'd all learned so much since camp started a few days ago. Out in the Alaskan wilderness, Nita felt like she could conquer anything. She had never seen any place like Alaska. The sky was bright blue. The air was the cleanest she'd ever smelled. The mountains were fierce and majestic.

Today was their final challenge. The one that would determine the winner of the prize money.

Nita was sure she was one of the best explorers in the group. She'd done great in both the ice climbing and ice cave challenges the day before. All she needed to do now was ace this last one.

"Before we issue our last challenge, I need everyone to gather over here so we can check your gear and equipment!" Nessa, the head guide, called.

Nita practically jumped up and down. She couldn't wait.

"Ready to lose, Nita?" a voice nearby asked.

Nita didn't even have to look around to know who that voice belonged to. Sohail had been competitive and rude ever since they'd arrived.

"In your dreams," she told him.

Nita trekked up to the front of the group. Sohail stayed right next to her. He always stayed at the front. It was like he wanted to absorb all the good explorer information for himself.

"Double-check your gear, everyone," Nessa called. "Your crampons first! Then, your ice axes, harnesses, helmets, and trekking poles."

Nita checked all her gear. She plodded through the snow, monster-style, in her crampons. She hit the snow with her ice ax and trekking pole.

When everyone was done, Nessa addressed the group again. "All right! We have something really fun planned for you today," she said. "For your final challenge, we're going to perform a partner wilderness exploration."

Nita quivered with excitement. She couldn't wait to find out who her partner would be.

"We'll be considering each explorer's accomplishments in order to determine our winner," Nessa continued. "We'll look at how you participated in all the challenges. And that includes how you work with a partner."

The guide paused and smiled. "The super fun part?" she said. "You'll complete this challenge without guides."

Nita's chest filled up with hope. She was going to *nail* it as an explorer. That prize money was hers.

"We're assigning groups of two," Nessa continued. "Each group will start out at a different point somewhere in this area. We'll have five different routes, but all the routes will lead to a cabin down the river. That's where we'll meet up."

Mr. Lorrain, one of the other guides, started reading the partners from a list.

Nita listened anxiously for her own name. But her heart dropped when Mr. Lorrain said, "Sohail Aman and Nita Dara!"

CHAPTER 2

PARTNERS

Nita couldn't believe it. She frowned at Sohail. Of all the rotten luck.

Nita looked at the guides to see if they were kidding. There was no way they'd missed Sohail giving her a hard time all week. She wasn't sure if he was just a jerk or competitive—or both. Either way, she didn't have time for it.

But it didn't seem to be a joke. Nessa was helping someone with their harness. Mr. Lorrain was talking with the other guides.

Nita sighed. Then she plunged her ice ax into the snow.

This challenge decides everything, she told herself. *No time to get distracted. Sohail had better not get in my way.*

"You'd better not ruin this," she muttered to him.

"*Me?*" Sohail said. "What about you—"

"All right everyone, let's move into our groups!" Mr. Lorrain interrupted. "Stand by your partner. A guide will come by and explain your route to you."

Nessa trekked over through the snow. She smiled at Nita and Sohail.

"Hi there!" Nessa said. She pulled out a map. "You two will be crossing the north side of this glacier. The glacier will slope down on the other side, onto the shore. You'll find a kayak waiting for you. You'll take the kayak down the river a few miles to the cabins. If you run into any trouble, set off a flare. You have several packed in your bags."

Nita couldn't help smiling. They'd already learned all the skills they'd need to complete this journey. Since arriving, they'd taken lessons in ice climbing, rappelling, glacier hiking, and sea kayaking. This challenge was going to be a piece of cake.

"I'll take you to your starting point," Nessa said. She led them farther away from the group until they couldn't see anyone else.

Once they were out of sight, she helped Nita and Sohail check their ropes and harnesses. They had learned that when hiking across a glacier, it was very important for hikers to wear harnesses and to be tied to the same rope. It was a precaution in case one person fell into a crevasse.

Crevasses were terrifying. They were huge, long, deep cracks in glaciers. If someone fell into a crevasse, it was up to the rest of the team to pull that person out. The explorers had practiced crevasse rescue just yesterday.

Nita managed to rope up by herself. She was using a kiwi coil, which meant the rope coiled across her chest and one shoulder, like a sash. Then it hooked into her harness. Sohail used the same technique.

"Good job, Nita," Nessa said, checking the knots. Then she checked Sohail's knots. "Um, you might have to redo yours, Sohail."

Nita tried not to smile. She was already coming out ahead.

Nessa said, "All ready! Straight in that direction. We're rooting for you!" And then she was gone.

Nita took a deep breath. *Even if I have the most annoying partner here, I'm still going to have fun—and win.*

"Well, let's go," Sohail said.

The pair set off across the glacier. The bottoms of their crampons were like spears on the hard surface.

Sohail led the way, using his trekking poles to stay steady on the snow and ice. Fresh, cool air hit his face.

They kept the rope loose between them, like they'd been told—not too much slack and not too tight.

Tingles of excitement went up and down Nita's spine as she walked. It was the first independent Explorer mission! She was so glad they'd saved it for last. It was going to be the most fun.

The wide, white expanse of the glacier spread out ahead of them. Nita couldn't get over how magical it looked, like a crystal kingdom. Or like a landscape on the moon. Some parts of the glacier looked like melted ice cream. Other parts were jagged and rippled. Some parts were smooth.

"This is pretty cool," Sohail said from in front of her.

"Yeah," Nita agreed. She looked into the distance as she walked.

The other side of the glacier looked like it was about a million miles away. Somewhere just beyond it, a kayak was waiting to take them down the river.

And I'll claim that prize money, Nita thought.

Nita listened to Sohail's slowly plodding feet ahead of her. She was starting to get impatient.

"Can't you go any faster?" Nita called up to him.

"No." Sohail turned and frowned. "Glaciers are dangerous. I'm not going to mess this up just because *you* want to go quicker."

Nita was surprised to hear him say that. During practice, Sohail always acted like nothing scared him.

For a while, Nita was quiet. She and Sohail kept trekking together in silence.

But Nita was getting mad. At this rate, they'd never reach the other side before the others.

"Look," Nita finally said, "I'm here to win. So you might want to pick up the pace a little!"

"Oh and you think *I* don't want the prize money too?" Sohail snapped. "Everyone needs the money, Nita. That's why we're here!"

Nita was about to answer when she noticed dark clouds rolling in over the sun. It happened so fast it was shocking. A chill struck the air. The temperature felt like it dropped by ten degrees.

Nita stopped. "Whoa," she said.

"It might snow," said Sohail. He sounded worried.

Nita was worried too. Their guides had stressed how fast the weather could change on the glacier when they first arrived. It could be dangerous.

A wall of fog started rolling toward them. It was the thickest fog Nita had ever seen. Within seconds, they could barely see a thing.

CHAPTER 3

IN THE FOG

"Are you still there?" Sohail's nervous voice came from ahead.

Nita could only see glimpses of him, when the fog shifted. "Where would I go?" she said. "I'm tied to you."

"The fog might go away in a minute," Sohail said. "Let's just wait and see if it passes."

Nita was even angrier now. Now the stupid fog was slowing them down too. And she didn't want to admit it, but she was scared. The fog was so thick and had moved so fast. It almost felt alive.

"Should we call for Nessa?" said Sohail.

"No!" Nita said. "We'll lose if they have to come rescue us. We can do this. We'll just wait."

They waited for a while longer, but the fog didn't seem to be stopping. Nita grew impatient.

"Let's just keep going—really slowly, though," she said.

They moved forward. Nita shuffled behind Sohail. She batted at the thick fog, but it didn't help. The whole world was gray now, like someone had covered it in a blanket.

"Maybe we're close to the edge of the glacier," Nita said, shivering. She couldn't tell anymore which direction they were going or where the other side of the glacier was. "I can't see where I'm—whoa!"

From in front of her, Nita felt a sudden hard tug on the rope. Then she heard a *crack!*

"Sohail?" she called.

"Falling!" his voice shouted.

Without thinking, Nita dropped flat on her stomach onto the snow, just as she'd been taught. The guides had taught them to self-arrest, in case another hiker fell. She kicked her feet into the snow, anchoring them there.

Nita clung to the ground, terrified. In the fog, they hadn't been able to see where they were going, and Sohail had given the signal: "Falling!"

That meant he'd fallen into a crevasse. Now Nita's body weight was the only thing stopping him from falling in farther.

CHAPTER 4

OVER THE EDGE!

"Sohail!" Nita shouted again.

"Be careful!" he yelled back from down below. "Don't fall in too!"

Nita lay there in the snow, her whole body pounding with fear. She tried desperately to remember what else she'd learned about crevasse rescue. But her brain was too jumbled to think clearly.

Still on her stomach, Nita scooted around to face the other direction. The fog was as thick as soup now, rolling over them, making it impossible to see.

"Is it really deep?" Nita called to Sohail.

"I'm not too far down!" he called back, his voice still muffled. "But the ice might crack!"

Nita's heart started pounding. She would need to haul Sohail out of the crevasse. Her mouth felt dry.

You can do this, she told herself. *Just think clearly.*

Nita tried not to move too much as she slipped her pack off her back and rooted around inside it. She had three pickets, two ice axes, two pulleys, cordelettes, and sling ropes. She also had more than a dozen carabiners—big, metal clips that glacier hikers seemed to use for almost everything.

"Don't worry, Sohail!" Nita yelled down to her partner.

Nita was sweating as she stared at her materials, trying her best to remember what they'd learned.

The first thing to do was make an anchor—something solid Nita could tie her rope to. Then she'd have to transfer Sohail's weight to the anchor, so that it wasn't just her holding him up.

Nita clipped her rope onto the picket and dug a deep T-shaped trench in the snow with her ice ax. The digging seemed to take forever, and Nita was shivering. She tried not to think about how scared Sohail must be right then.

Finally the trench was deep enough. Nita set the picket on its side in the T-trench and buried it with snow so that only the rope was sticking out. Then she attached her rope to the anchor.

I need a backup anchor too, in case the first one fails, Nita remembered.

Still shivering, she used her second picket to make another anchor. Then she attached one of the pulleys to the rope, tying the two anchors together.

With Sohail's weight transferred to the anchors, Nita finally felt safe enough to stand. She approached the edge of the crevasse. There was Sohail, wedged inside, looking up at her helplessly.

"Hold on!" Nita called.

She took a deep, shaky breath. She wasn't sure if she'd done everything right. There were so many steps, and she was half-numb with fear. But it was time to see if her pulley system worked.

"Pulling now!" she called.

Nita started pulling the rope back up toward the anchor. Her arms felt like they were on fire, and she was sweating with the effort. Even though Sohail said he hadn't dropped down too far, he was heavy.

Finally Sohail's head appeared, followed by the rest of him. He scrambled to get over the edge.

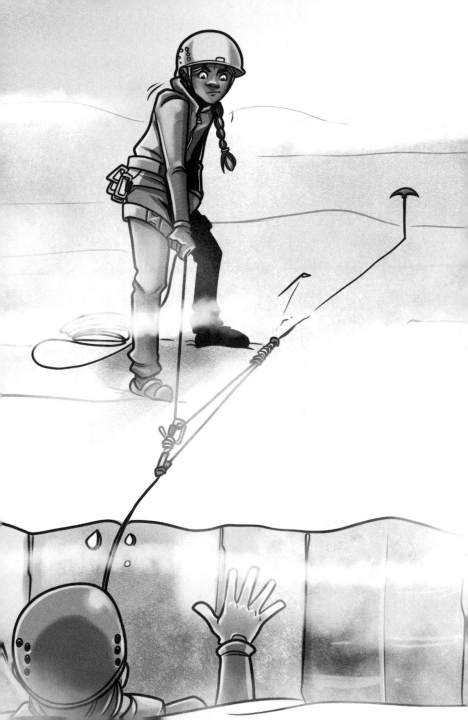

With a loud grunt, Sohail made it out of the crevasse and back onto the glacier. He wiggled forward on his belly, moving far away from the edge.

"You did it! You saved me!" Sohail said breathlessly. He glanced at the pulley system, anchored deep in the ice. "I can't believe you remembered how to do all this stuff!"

"I can't believe it either," Nita panted. She was sweating inside her snowsuit and still shaking.

Sohail lay back in the snow, panting. His breath was quick and shallow. It seemed to take forever for him to start breathing normally again.

Finally he rolled over on his side and checked his watch. "We've been out here for almost two hours," he said. "Let's get moving. Maybe there's still a chance we can win."

"We can take our time," Nita replied, still shaken. For once, she didn't want to hurry. "I still can't see anything in this fog anyway."

Sohail nodded. Together, they dug the anchor out of the ice and rolled up the ropes.

"I don't know how far the other side of the glacier is," Nita said. The fog was still as thick as smoke.

"We've got to be close," Sohail said. He shivered. "Let's get moving."

They packed up their gear and kept moving. But this time, they went on their hands and knees.

Nita crawled behind Sohail, using a trekking pole to test the ground ahead. It was uncomfortable crawling with only one hand, but she didn't dare stand up. She was not going to fall into a crevasse too. The next one might be one of those deep pits that seemed to slice right into the middle of the earth.

"I don't know if this is a good idea or not," Nita called up to him.

"I don't either," Sohail admitted. He sounded a bit unsure. "But it feels safer than walking."

They kept crawling along the glacier, checking carefully for crevasses.

To distract herself, Nita asked, "So why do you need the prize money?"

Sohail didn't answer at first. Then he called back, "My family and I are refugees. We came to America from Syria a few years ago, to escape the war there. I have three younger siblings. In Syria, my father was a businessman. Here he's a driver for a car company. He's still learning English and doesn't make much money. It's hard."

He paused, then said, "My family is depending on me. I need the money for all of us."

Nita felt her heart twist. She kept her eyes down on the snow. She hadn't thought of Sohail as someone who needed the money as much as she did.

"What about you?" Sohail said. "Why do you need the money?"

Nita still didn't look up. She swept her own trekking pole around before she scooted forward.

"I live with my Aunt Carmen," she said. "She raised me. She's a housekeeper, so she doesn't make much either. I need the money for stuff like school supplies. And so our water doesn't keep getting shut off."

This time Sohail didn't answer. Nita wondered if he was also thinking that they were more alike than he'd realized.

The fog was letting up. The world was still gray, but they were starting to be able to see.

"I think we're close to the edge of the glacier," Sohail said, standing up.

Nita almost shouted with relief. Sohail was right. The massive field of ice and snow seemed to be coming to an end.

"The slope should be right here," Sohail said, excited. "Our kayak awaits!"

Nita stood too. She couldn't wait to be down on the beach. She was careful to go slowly as they approached the edge.

Suddenly she stopped short. "Whoa!" Nita gasped.

The drop down to the ground was sharp and sudden. They'd reached the edge of the glacier and were looking down at a solid, vertical wall of ice that plunged to the shore.

At the bottom of the glacier wall was the beach and then the river. There wasn't a kayak anywhere.

CHAPTER 5

A WALL OF ICE

Sohail looked at Nita. They were both clearly thinking the same thing: *We're doomed.*

"I don't see that easy slope leading off the glacier," Nita said, looking around. "Didn't Nessa say it would be here? And where's our kayak?"

Sohail scanned the beach below, his face scrunched up with worry. "We might have gotten turned around in the fog and come to the wrong part of the glacier," he said. "Our kayak must be farther down the beach."

Nita looked around. There was a hill to the left—no getting off the glacier that way. And there was still a thick fog to the right. It was impossible to see where the slope might be.

Nita pictured crawling along the top of the glacier in that fog, and her heart sank. "I have an idea," she said, trying to sound brave. "We learned ice climbing and rappelling. Why don't we just rappel down this wall?"

Rappelling involved securing a rope to the top of a cliff or mountain and then going down the side of the cliff attached to the rope. It was one of the first skills they'd covered when they'd arrived in Alaska.

But Sohail looked even more worried. "This one's really steep," he said. "Steeper than the walls we practiced on."

"I think we should try it," Nita said, her confidence growing. "I'd rather rappel than keep being scared of falling in a crevasse."

Sohail clearly didn't like it, but Nita was already getting her gear ready. She took out her ax and picket again and dug a T-trench in the snow. The T-shaped ditch would make a good anchor for rappelling.

Sohail didn't bother arguing. He helped bury Nita's picket in the trench and secure it, so that it would bear their weight.

"Do you think it'll hold?" Nita asked. Suddenly the glacier wall did look like a long way down.

"Yeah," Sohail said. But he still looked worried.

When Nita's rope was securely tied to the anchor and her harness, she started rappelling over the edge. She used both ice axes to steady herself.

Smack, smack! The axes went into the ice, lodging themselves deep into the glacier wall.

The ice and snow slipped and crumbled under Nita's feet. Then, for some reason, one of the axes wouldn't grab hold of the ice.

"What's wrong?" came Sohail's voice.

Nita looked up at his worried face, then down to the bottom of the glacier. "I don't know, my ax isn't grabbing the—"

Before she knew it, her feet had slipped. Nita dropped one of the axes and screamed.

CHAPTER 6

ON SOLID GROUND

Nita dangled there in her harness, terrified, swinging on the rope. For a second she forgot the ropes were there and panicked, scrambling to grab the ice.

"Stop panicking!" cried Sohail. "Stay calm! The anchor's secure! Just rappel down!"

"*You* try staying calm!" Nita cried.

"You can do this!" Sohail said. "You don't even need your axes to go down!"

Nita tried to listen to his voice rather than her own fear. She lowered herself the rest of the way down.

When she finally got down to the snowy beach, she collapsed. Sweat was pouring down her face.

"I can't believe I made it," Nita gasped.

Up above, Sohail cheered. He unhooked the rope from the anchor and threw it down. Then he hooked his own harness to the anchor.

"Coming!" he called.

Nita watched her partner rappel over the side. She held her breath until he made it all the way down.

Once they were both on solid ground, Nita and Sohail let out identical cheers of relief. Their voices echoed off the glacier wall.

"I kind of never want to see a glacier again," Nita said.

"I know how you feel," Sohail said, unhooking the rope from his harness. He glanced up with a sad expression. "We'll have to leave the anchor up there."

"That's OK," Nita said. "Let's just find our kayak!"

Now that they were on the beach, Nita was thinking about the prize money again. *Maybe the fog slowed everybody else down too,* she thought. *We might have a chance!*

Nita and Sohail hurried down the shore along the river, looking for the kayak.

"I think I see it. Up there!" Sohail said, pointing.

Nita squinted. Sure enough, she could see something long and bright yellow moored on the shore up ahead. But before they'd made it much farther, a clap of thunder shook the air.

Both kids looked up and frowned. Clouds scudded over the sky again. But this time it wasn't fog. A storm was coming!

CHAPTER 7

WATER AND STORM!

"You've got to be kidding me," said Sohail, staring up at the clouds.

"Hurry!" Nita cried. "Maybe we can make it down the river before the storm hits!"

Things didn't look good. Dark clouds were already blanketing a huge part of the sky. Together, Nita and Sohail hurried as fast as they could toward the two-person kayak.

As they reached the kayak and jumped in, rain started to fall. It was the coldest rain Nita and Sohail had ever felt. Some of the raindrops felt like ice.

"Freezing rain!" Sohail said.

Nita grabbed a paddle. They pushed off into the river, paddling as fast as possible.

"Oh no—look!" Sohail cried.

Nita looked toward the glacier on the left. A huge gush of water came roaring out from between two icy crags and surged into the river.

"Meltwater!" Sohail shouted.

The river rose and swelled up as the meltwater poured into it. A big spray splashed up into Nita's face. She sputtered but gripped the paddle tightly.

"Paddle faster!" she shouted. "It could flood the kayak!"

The kids dug in with their paddles, and the kayak swerved between rocks and floating bits of ice. The clouds overhead grew even thicker and darker. A bright band of lightning flashed in the sky.

"I don't know how long it'll be safe to stay in the water!" Sohail said. More thunder rumbled.

The kayak barely missed some of the high, jagged rocks along the river's edge. The sky flashed with more lightning. More thunder sounded. It was closer now.

"We have to get out of the water!" Sohail yelled.

Nita could only nod in agreement.

Just then, the swelling river sent the kayak crashing into one of the larger rocks near the shore. Nita and Sohail slammed against it.

Nita reached out and grabbed onto the rock. She hung on as best she could while the water rushed around them.

"Come on!" Sohail yelled. He scrambled out of his seat and onto the rock.

Nita followed, slipping on the rock as she crawled. Together, she and Sohail grabbed the kayak and managed to drag it onto the shore.

"We need to find shelter—fast," Sohail said. Heavy rain pounded his helmet and jacket.

The two teens hurried farther onto the shore, hauling the kayak behind them. There was no shelter in sight.

"What about right here?" Sohail said. He pointed toward a narrow passage between two rocky hills.

"There are no caves or anything," Nita said, looking around.

"We could try turning the kayak upside down there," Sohail suggested. "If we use it as a roof, it would keep us dry."

Nita nodded. "Let's try it," she said.

Together the two explorers hoisted the kayak into the air, turning it upside down. Then they wedged it across the alley between the two rocky hills. Now it was a narrow roof. There was just enough room underneath for them to sit.

"Come on," Sohail said.

The thunder sounded again, even closer now. Nita crawled under the kayak, just as lightning struck close by.

CHAPTER 8

SHELTER

Nita and Sohail huddled under their new shelter. The ground rumbled, and the freezing rain pounded the top of the kayak. They tried to make themselves as tiny as possible.

"It's OK, they'll come find us," Sohail said. He sounded like he was trying to convince himself as much as Nita.

Nita hugged her pack to her chest. She hoped the lightning wouldn't slither down between these two rocky hills and find them.

"Our flares! We could set them!" Sohail said suddenly.

He pulled them out of his bag, then hesitated. "They probably won't see them in this storm, though," he said.

"Yeah . . . maybe we should wait to send them then," Nita said.

They didn't say anything after that, just huddled there together. They'd been out on their own for hours now. Nita didn't want to say what she was thinking: hypothermia.

Their guides had warned them about how dangerous hypothermia could be. If people got freezing cold and wet, their body temperatures dropped too much.

"I really wanted to win that prize money," Nita finally said in a small voice.

"I wanted to win too," Sohail said. "But let's just focus on trying not to freeze."

Nita took a deep breath and said words she never thought she'd say. "You know what? If I do win, I'll—I'll split the money with you."

Sohail turned to stare. "Are you serious?" he said.

Nita bit her lip and nodded. "Yeah. We could both use it. Even half the prize money would help both our families a lot."

Sohail kept staring. A slow smile spread across his face. "I'll make the same promise. If I win, I'll split it with you too."

Nita smiled. Then she half-laughed. "If we don't freeze to death."

"True." Sohail's teeth were chattering. "All right. I don't think we should wait. I'm going to set the flare and hope they see it."

Without waiting for a reply, Sohail crawled out from under the kayak. He set the flare and raced back.

Nita watched it burn a bright red in the rain. It was mesmerizing. And she was so, so tired. She put her head on her knees and closed her eyes.

Sohail shook her shoulder roughly. "Stay awake!" he warned. "It's dangerous to fall asleep when you're this cold!"

Nita knew he was right. It was one of the risks of hypothermia. It was hard, but she forced herself to keep her eyes open.

And then, a little while later, they saw it—a sleek, narrow helicopter, lowering itself down on the beach in front of them!

CHAPTER 9

SAFE

Nita and Sohail scrambled out from under the kayak. Together they stumbled toward the chopper.

Mr. Lorrain and two medics came out and helped the kids in. Nita and Sohail quickly sat down and fastened their seatbelts, grateful to be out of the cold.

"Thank goodness you're both all right!" Mr. Lorrain said as the helicopter lifted into the sky. "The guides were able to locate the other teams pretty quickly once the fog rolled in. But you two were so off course they couldn't find you."

Nita was still shivering like crazy as the chopper rose above the river. Below she could see the wide, white glacier she and Sohail had crossed.

For much of their journey, the glacier had been hidden in fog. But now, from up here, Nita was reminded of how enormous it was. She couldn't believe they'd come all that way.

I'm glad Sohail was with me, she thought.

The helicopter flew a few miles down the shore to the cabins. The entire Alaska Young Explorers team was waiting. Everyone looked worried.

"Let's let them rest and recover!" Mr. Lorrain said.

The medics checked Sohail and Nita over. They made both kids take lukewarm baths, then wrapped them up in heated blankets.

Nita finally started to feel warm again. As she and Sohail sat there, wrapped up and sipping warm tea, the guides came to sit in the cabin living room with them.

"Why don't you tell us what happened," said Nessa.

Sohail and Nita glanced at each other. They were clearly both thinking the same thing: *Once they hear what a mess we made of our expedition, they'll kick us out.*

But they had to tell the truth.

Nita could barely look at the guides as she and Sohail explained what had happened out there.

The longer they talked, the sadder Nita felt. She pictured her aunt's face. Carmen would be so disappointed that Nita hadn't won the prize money.

Nita shot a look at Sohail. He clearly felt just as bad.

When they were done, the guides looked at each other. "Can you excuse us for a minute, guys?" Nessa said.

The guides went in the other room. Sohail and Nita looked at each other, clearly thinking the same thing: everything they'd worked for, gone in an instant.

"Do you think they'll kick us out?" Sohail asked nervously.

"I have no idea," said Nita.

When the guides came back, they looked serious. Nita's heart sank. They were about to be sent home.

Mr. Lorrain began, "As you know, certain guidelines must be followed for an Explorers challenge. One of those has always been that the winners need to finish first. But there are other requirements too. We look for Young Explorers who are quick thinking, courageous, and display good teamwork skills."

Sohail and Nita nodded glumly.

Nessa took over. "So this year, we've decided to change things up a bit," she said. "You kids have both been incredible. Despite the bad weather, you performed a crevasse rescue on your own. You rappelled the glacier wall and found safe shelter during the storm . . . all by yourselves!"

Nita let out a breath. She was confused. Nessa didn't look mad, but still . . . what did all that mean?

"We've been talking," Mr. Lorrain continued. "And we agree this is a very special circumstance. This challenge was originally set to determine one winner, but we've decided to award *two* prizes this year. You've both won the Alaska Young Explorers prize!"

Nita couldn't believe it. She stared at the guides. Then she looked at Sohail, whose eyes were as big as her own. Then she jumped up, still wrapped in the heated blanket.

"*Woo-hoo!*" she cried.

Sohail jumped up too, even though he looked like he was still in disbelief.

Nita hugged him. "We wouldn't have made it without each other," she said. She didn't care if it sounded cheesy. It was true. They made a good team.

"I know." Sohail's eyes were still huge with shock. "My dad will freak out when I tell him. I never win anything."

"Me neither," Nita admitted.

"Once the word gets out, the local news team might even want to interview you," Nessa said. "If your parents are all right with that."

Sohail sat back down in shock. "Us? They'd want to interview us?"

Nessa nodded. "Yes, for your courage and skill." She smiled. "Stuff like this doesn't happen every day."

"Excuse me," Nita told everyone. "I have a call to make."

She went to her room, got out her phone, and dialed the familiar number. She still felt dizzy from the adventure she'd survived.

"Nita?" Aunt Carmen answered the phone. "Are you all right?"

"Aunt Carmen?" Nita said. "Are you sitting down? Because you'll never, ever believe what happened. . . ."

AUTHOR BIO

Salima Alikhan has been a freelance writer and illustrator for fourteen years. She lives in Austin, Texas, where she writes and illustrates children's books. Her most recent project, *Emmi in the City: A Great Chicago Fire Survival Story*, was published in 2019 as part of Capstone's Girls Survive series. Salima also teaches creative writing at St. Edward's University and English at Austin Community College. Her books and art can be found online at www.salimaalikhan.net.

ILLUSTRATOR BIO

Alan Brown is an English illustrator working in children's books and comics. His love of art started as a young boy, when he had unlimited access to comics at his gran's sweetie shop. These days he can be found busy at his desk, illustrating with help from his two sons and dog.

GLOSSARY

competition (kahm-puh-TI-shuhn)—a contest between two or more people

crampon (KRAM-pahn)—a metal frame with pointed metal teeth that attaches to a climber's boot; crampons give climbers secure footing on snow and ice

crevasse (kri-VAS)—a deep, wide crack in a glacier or ice sheet

glacier (GLAY-shur)—a huge moving body of ice found in mountain valleys or polar regions

hypothermia (hye-puh-THUR-mee-uh)—a life-threatening condition that occurs when a person's body temperature falls several degrees below normal

ice ax (AHYS AKS)—a combination pick and cutting tool with a spiked handle that is used in mountain climbing

kayak (KYE-ak)—a small, narrow boat that holds one or two people and is moved by a paddle

meltwater (MELT-waw-tur)—water that comes from the melting of ice and snow

picket (PIK-it)—a pointed or sharpened stake or post

pulley (PUL-ee)—a grooved wheel turned by a rope, belt, or chain that often moves heavy objects

rappel (ruh-PEL)—to slide down a strong rope

refugee (ref-yuh-JEE)—a person forced to flee his or her home because of natural disaster or war

scholarship (SKOL-ur-ship)—a grant or prize that pays for a student to go to college or to follow a course of study

DISCUSSION QUESTIONS

1. What other stories do you know about people trying to survive in the wilderness? Talk about movies, books, and TV shows that have given you information about being in the wild. Do you think you would make it in the wilderness? Why or why not?

2. Why do you think Nita and Sohail didn't like each other very much at first? Talk about how their relationship changed. How did they come to understand and like each other better?

3. Nita and Sohail both talked about why they needed to win the prize money. How are their home lives different from kids whose families have enough money?

WRITING PROMPTS

1. Nita and Sohail had to learn all about the snowy, icy weather in Alaska. Have you ever been to a place with a very different climate than what you're used to? Write a paragraph about what those differences were. If not, write a paragraph about where you would like to go that's different from other places you've been.

2. Nita and Sohail both feel strongly that they need to win the Explorers competition. Have you ever been part of a competition you really wanted to win? Why did you want to win so badly? Write a paragraph explaining your reasons.

3. What do you think would have happened if Sohail and Nita had both fallen into the crevasse? Rewrite Chapter 4 to reflect that situation.

MORE ABOUT OUTDOOR ADVENTURES

Despite glaciers making up a large part of our planet, many people don't realize how gigantic they truly are. Glaciers are huge bodies of ice and snow that move on their own. Some of them are so massive you can see them from space!

- To be considered a real glacier, it must be at least twenty-five square acres. That's the size of nearly nineteen football fields!

- Some glaciers look blue because that's the only color glacial ice can't absorb. The dense ice of the glacier absorbs every other color—so blue is what we see!

- Right now, the largest glacier on Earth is Lambert Glacier in Antarctica. It's sixty miles wide and approximately 270 miles long.

- There are around 100,000 glaciers in Alaska alone.

Glacier hiking trips are a great way to explore these massive ice fields. People can glacier hike no matter how old they are. Ice climbing, kayaking, and exploring ice caves and lagoons can also be done on glaciers.

Ice climbing is when people climb on ice formations like glacier walls and frozen waterfalls. Ice-climbing competitions started in Russia and have been held there every winter since 1970. In March of 2019, two ice climbers made it to the top of Canada's highest waterfall, Della Falls, which is 1,443 feet high!

Kayaking is a fun activity that people can do in warm or cold waters. When kayaks were first invented, they were made of seal or other animal skin stretched over wood or whale bone. Kayaks are very quiet, which made them perfect for hunting and sneaking up on prey. Now, they are perfect for gliding quietly through the water and spotting wildlife.